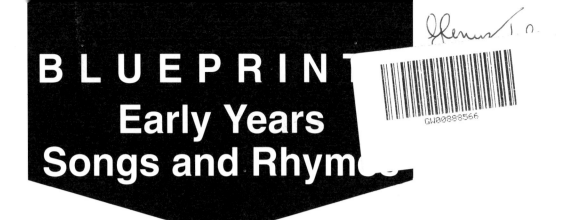

BLUEPRINT
Early Years
Songs and Rhymes

Compiled by Liz Withers

Stanley Thornes (Publishers) Ltd

Do you receive *BLUEPRINTS NEWS*?

Blueprints is an expanding series of practical teacher's ideas books and photocopiable resources for use in primary schools. Books are available for separate infant and junior age ranges for every core and foundation subject, as well as for an ever widening range of other primary teaching needs. These include **Blueprints Primary English** books and **Blueprints Resource Banks**. **Blueprints** are carefully structured around the demands of National Curriculum in England and Wales, but are used successfully by schools and teachers in Scotland, Northern Ireland and elsewhere.

Blueprints provide :
- *Total curriculum coverage*
- *Hundreds of practical ideas*
- *Books specifically for the age range you teach*
- *Flexible resources for the whole school or for individual teachers*
- *Excellent photocopiable sheets - ideal for assessment and children's work profiles*
- *Supreme value*

Books may be bought by credit card over the telephone and information obtained on **(0242) 228485.** Alternatively, photocopy and return this **FREEPOST** form to receive **Blueprints News**, our regular update on all new and existing titles. You may also like to add the name of a friend who would be interested in being on the mailing list.

Please add my name to the **BLUEPRINTS NEWS** mailing list.

Mr/Mrs/Miss/Ms --

Home address --

---Postcode -------------------------

School address --

-- Postcode -------------------------

Please also send **BLUEPRINTS NEWS** to :

Mr/Mrs/Miss/Ms --

Address --

-- Postcode -------------------------

To: Marketing Services Dept., Stanley Thornes Ltd, FREEPOST (GR 782), Cheltenham, GL50 1BR

Introduction, selection and notes © Liz Withers 1994
Original line illustrations by Debbie Clark © ST(P) Ltd 1994

First published in 1994 by:
Stanley Thornes (Publishers) Ltd
Ellenborough House
Wellington Street
CHELTENHAM GL50 1YD

A catalogue record for this book is available from the British Library.
ISBN 0–7487–1732–3

Typeset by Tech-Set, Gateshead, Tyne & Wear
Printed and bound in Great Britain

CONTENTS

Contents

Side 2

Cassette contents

INTRODUCTION

Early Years Songs and Rhymes aims to provide a compendium of all the nursery rhymes, finger rhymes, action rhymes, and songs that early years teachers will want to have in their classroom repertoire. It includes some that will be new and unfamiliar as well as all the classic songs and rhymes. It is intended to be used widely in nursery classes, playgroups and primary schools, by teachers, students and parents who want to learn, teach or accompany rhymes and songs with children.

For all those items that include music, you will find a straightforward piano arrangement plus guitar chords. For those who do not have access to music accompaniment or playing abilities, the *Early Years Songs and Rhymes* cassettes will prove invaluable. These provide accompaniment-only versions of all songs, nearly 150 minutes of music in all. You can use them either with the children in the classroom, or to teach yourself a new song before introducing it to the children.

You can locate all songs on the cassettes by this logo in the book, which appears in the song titles:

You will also find that all the actions in action songs have been clearly and simply explained with italicised instructions. Many teachers may like to teach or use these songs and rhymes alongside topics they are working on with their children. For this reason we have included a simple topic index on page vii to help you locate suitable material.

ACKNOWLEDGEMENTS

I would like to thank Tracey Renwick for enthusiastically arranging the music for me. Stephen Keeley has typeset the music, and I was very grateful for his suggestion for the inclusion of music for the guitar. There are very few playgroups equipped with a piano, but often a teacher or parent-helper has hidden talents as a guitarist. This adds a new dimension with percussion instruments at rhyme and singing time!

I do hope you will continue to enjoy the traditional rhymes and songs, but also have fun introducing the children to some of the more unfamiliar ones included here.

Liz Withers

The publishers gratefully acknowledge permission to reproduce the following copyright material in the book and cassette:

'Three Naughty Kittens' (printed music) by Peter Canwell © Copyright 1987 Peter Canwell, reproduced by permission of Music Sales Ltd, London W1; Peter Canwell for 'Three Naughty Kittens' (cassette); 'The Dice Song' by Harriet Powell and 'The Dinosaur's Feeling Hungry' by Charlie Stafford and the children of Quarry Hill Flats, Leeds from 'Game Songs with Prof Dogg's Troupe' published by A & C Black (publishers) Limited; Stainer & Bell Ltd for 'Little Arabella Miller' by Ann Elliott; 'The Hokey Cokey' © Copyright 1942 Kennedy Music Co Ltd, England, Campbell Connelly & Co Ltd, 8–9 Frith Street, London W1V 5TZ for the world, used by permission, all rights reserved; 'Postman Pat' (printed music) by Bryan Daly © 1994 Post Music reproduced with permission of Chester Music Ltd; 'Postman Pat' (cassette) © 1994 Post Music reproduced with permission of Post Music.

The publishers have made every attempt to trace copyright holders of the following items but have been unable to do so; 'Six Little Ducks'; 'The Ants went Marching'; 'I have got an Engine' by David Moses; 'I Love to Row in my Big Blue Boat' by J B Cramer.

TOPIC INDEX

NURSERY RHYMES

Side 1A

1. BAA-BAA BLACK SHEEP

Baa – baa black sheep, have you an–y wool? Yes sir, yes sir, three bags full.

One for the Mas – ter and one for the Dame, And one for the lit-tle boy that lives down the lane.

 Side 1A

2. HUMPTY DUMPTY

Hump-ty Dump-ty sat on the wall, Hump-ty Dump-ty had a great fall,

All the King's hor-ses and all the King's men, Could-n't put Hump-ty to - geth-er a - gain.

3. SING A SONG OF SIXPENCE

Sing a song of six - pence, a poc - ket full of rye, Four and twen - ty

black - birds ba - ked in a pie, When the pie was o - pen the

birds be - gan to sing, Now was - n't that a dain - ty dish to set be - fore the King.

4. LITTLE JACK HORNER

Lit - tle Jack Hor - ner, Sat in the cor - ner, Eat - ing his Christ - mas pie._____ He

put in his thumb and pulled out a plum, And said, what a good boy am I.

4

5. TWINKLE, TWINKLE LITTLE STAR

6. HICKORY, DICKORY DOCK

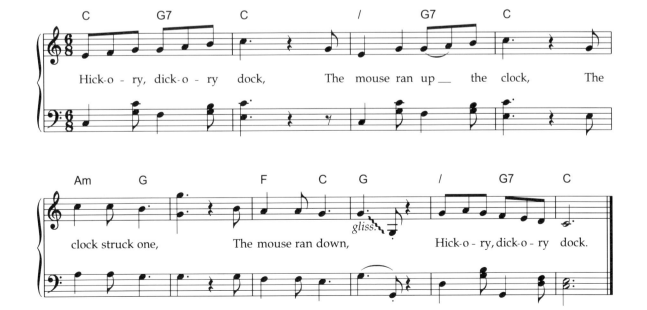

Side 1A — 7. I HAD A LITTLE NUT-TREE

I had a lit-tle nut-tree, no-thing would it bear, but a sil-ver nut-meg and a gold-en pear, The King of Spain's Daugh-ter, Came to vi-sit me, all for the sake of my lit-tle nut-tree.

Side 1A — 8. JACK AND JILL WENT UP THE HILL

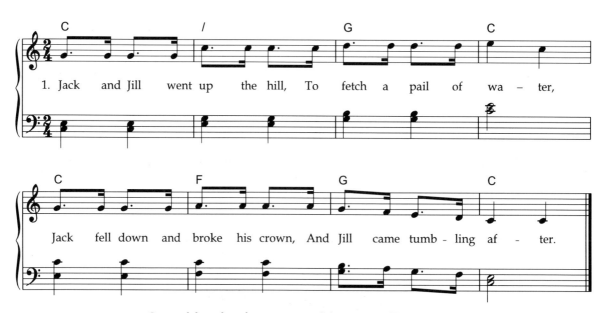

1. Jack and Jill went up the hill, To fetch a pail of wa-ter, Jack fell down and broke his crown, And Jill came tumb-ling af-ter.

v.2 Up Jack got and home did trot
As fast as he could caper,
He went to bed to mend his head
With vinegar and brown paper.

6

Side 1A   9. PUSSY CAT, PUSSY CAT

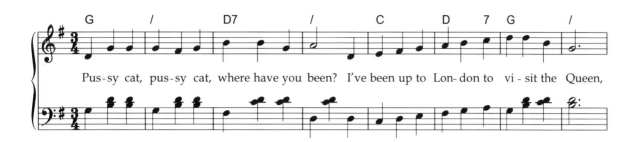

Pus-sy cat, pus-sy cat, where have you been? I've been up to Lon-don to vi-sit the Queen,

Pus-sy cat, pus-sy cat, what did you there? I frigh-tened a lit-tle mouse un-der her chair.

Side 1A   10. LITTLE MISS MUFFET

Lit-tle Miss Muf-fet sat on a tuf-fet, Eat-ing her curds and whey,_____ There

came a big spi-der who sat down be-side her, And frigh-tened Miss Muf-fet a - way.

Side 1A

11. OLD MOTHER HUBBARD

1. Old Moth-er Hub-bard, she went to the cup-board, To fetch her poor dog — a bone, —

When she got there, the cup-board was bare, and so the poor dog — had none.

Verses 2-4

She went to the ba-ker to buy him some bread, but when she got back the poor dog was dead.

v.3   She went to the joiner to buy him a coffin,
But when she got back the poor dog was laughing.

v.4   The dame made a curtsey, the dog made a bow,
The dame said, 'Your servant', the dog said, 'Bow-wow'.

8

Side 1A

12. SEE SAW MARGERY DAW

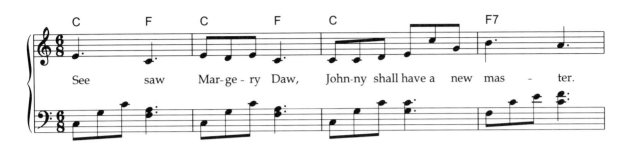

See saw Mar-ge-ry Daw, John-ny shall have a new mas - ter.

He shall have but a pen-ny a day, Be - cause he can't go an-y fas - ter.

 Side 1A

13. HEY DIDDLE DIDDLE

Hey did-dle did-dle, the cat and the fid-dle, The cow jumped o-ver the moon, The

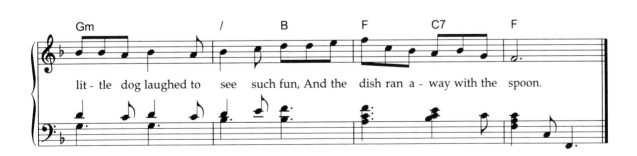

lit-tle dog laughed to see such fun, And the dish ran a-way with the spoon.

14. SIMPLE SIMON
Side 1A

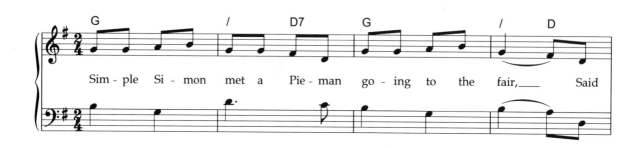

Sim - ple Si - mon met a Pie - man go - ing to the fair,___ Said

Sim - ple Si - mon to the Pie - man, "Let me taste your ware".

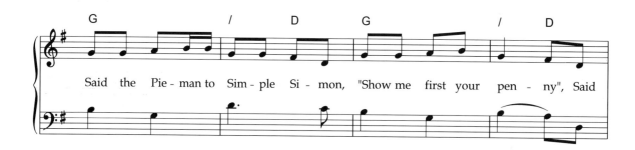

Said the Pie - man to Sim - ple Si - mon, "Show me first your pen - ny", Said

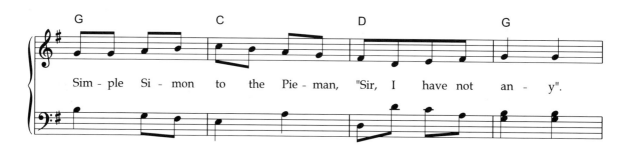

Sim - ple Si - mon to the Pie - man, "Sir, I have not an - y".

15. LITTLE BOY BLUE
Side 1A

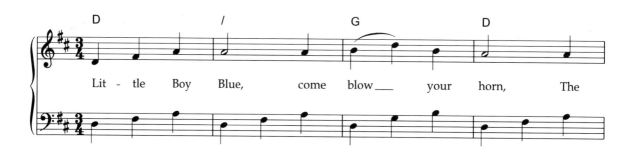

Lit - tle Boy Blue, come blow___ your horn, The

10

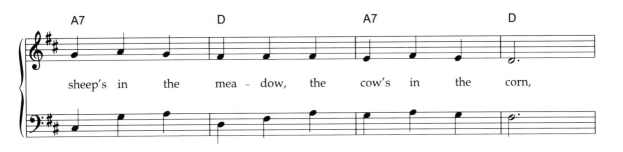

sheep's in the mea - dow, the cow's in the corn,

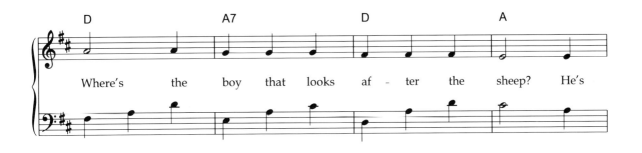

Where's the boy that looks af - ter the sheep? He's

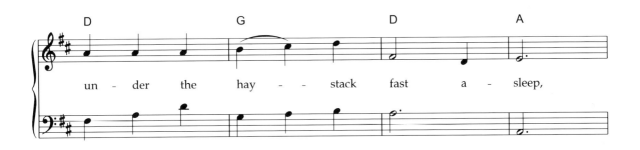

un - der the hay - - stack fast a - sleep,

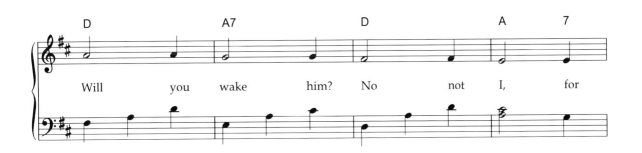

Will you wake him? No not I, for

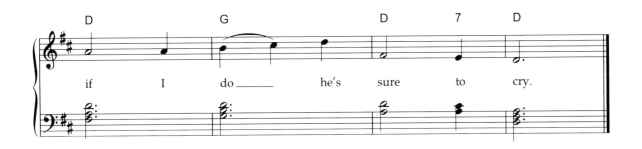

if I do ____ he's sure to cry.

11

Side 1A

16. FRÈRE JACQUES

Frè - re   Ja - ques,   Frè - re   Ja - ques,   dor - mez - vous?   dor - mez - vous?

Son-nez les ma-ti - nes,   son-nez les ma-ti - nes,   Ding, dang dong,   Ding, dang   dong.

Side 1A

17. HUSH-A-BYE BABY

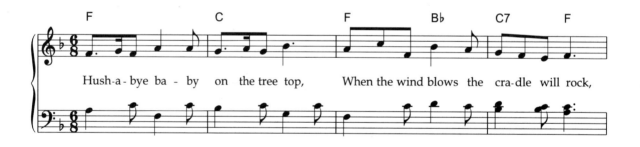

Hush-a- bye ba - by   on the tree top,   When the wind blows the cra-dle will rock,

When the bough breaks the cra-dle will fall,   Down will come ba - by,   cra-dle and all.

FINGER AND ACTION RHYMES

1. THE BEE

1, 2, 3, – I can see a bee.
4 and 5 – flying to a hive.
6, 7, 8, – he's a little late.
9 and 10 – out he flies again.

2. THE BEEHIVE

Here is the beehive,
Where are the bees?
Hidden away where nobody sees.
Soon they are creeping out of the hive,
1, 2, 3, 4, 5.

3. AN ELEPHANT GOES LIKE THIS AND THAT

(Commence standing with both feet placed well apart.)
An elephant goes like this and that,
(Pat knees.)
He's terrible big,
(Hands up high.)
And he's terrible fat,
(Hands out wide.)
He has no fingers,
(Clench together.)
And he has no toes,
(Touch toes.)
But goodness gracious, what a nose!
(Make large movements simulating the trunk with the right hand and arm extended to the front, swaying gently from right side to left side. Repeat.)

4. JACK BE NIMBLE, JACK BE QUICK!

Jack be nimble, Jack be quick,
Jack jump over the candlestick.

*The children sit in a circle and the candlestick is placed in the centre.
The child is chosen by name and responds by jumping over the
candlestick and back again, before returning to his/her original place in
the circle.
The game is repeated using the name of a different child each time.*

5. BABIES

The hen has a little chick,
What does it say?
'Cheep, cheep, cheep, cheep!'
All through the day.

Duck – duckling – 'quack!'
Sheep – lamb – 'baa!'
Pig – piglet – 'squeak!'
Cat – kitten – 'meow!'
Dog – puppy – 'bow-wow!'
Snail – baby – it doesn't say
All through the day!

6. CAN YOU WALK ON TIPTOE?

Can you walk on tiptoe, softly as a cat?
Can you stamp along the road, stamp! stamp!,
Just like that?
Can you take some giant strides
Just like a giant can?
Or walk along so slowly like a poor, bent old man?

7. BUILD A HOUSE WITH FIVE BRICKS

Build a house with five bricks,
1, 2, 3, 4, 5.
Put a roof on top,
And a chimney too,
Where the wind blows through.

Place right clenched fist over the top of the left clenched fist. Remove left clenched fist and place on top of the right.
Repeat three times.
Touch fingertips to indicate the roof.
Touch two index fingers to indicate the chimney.
'Where the wind blows through.' Gently blow through touching index fingers.

8. FIVE LITTLE PEAS IN A PEA-POD PRESSED

Five little peas in a pea-pod pressed,
(Clench fingers on one hand.)
One grew, two grew and so did all the rest.
(Raise fingers slowly.)
They grew and grew and did not stop,
(Stretch fingers wide.)
Until one day the pod went POP!
(Clap loudly on 'pop.')

9. HERE IS A STEAMROLLER

Here is a steamroller, rolling and rolling,
Ever so slowly, because of its load.
Then it rolls up to the top of the hill,
Puffing and panting it has to stand still.
Then it rolls ... all the way down.

Roll fists round each other, slowly moving upwards, then down again very fast on the last line.

17

10. FIVE LITTLE MONKEYS WALKED ALONG THE SHORE

Five little monkeys walked along the shore,
One went a-sailing,
Then there were four.
Four little monkeys climbed up a tree,
One of them tumbled down,
Then there were three.
Three little monkeys found a pot of glue,
One got stuck in it,
Then there were two.
Two little monkeys found a currant bun,
One ran away with it,
Then there was one.
One little monkey cried all afternoon,
So they put him in an aeroplane
And sent him to the moon.

Use fingers to indicate the number of monkeys.

11. FIVE LITTLE LEAVES SO BRIGHT AND GAY

Five little leaves so bright and gay,
Were dancing about on a tree one day.
The wind came blowing through the town,
Ooooooooooooooo … ooooooooooo
One little leaf came tumbling down.

Four little leaves so bright and gay, etc.

Use fingers to represent leaves, and blow gently to make the noise of the wind. Or: use five children as leaves.

12. FIVE LITTLE MICE

Five little mice came out to play,
Gathering crumbs along the way,
Out comes a pussy-cat sleek and black,
Only four little mice went scampering back.
Four little mice …
Three little mice …
Two little mice …
One little mouse came out to play,
Gathering crumbs along the way,
Out comes a pussy-cat, sleek and black,
No little mice went scampering back.

13. MIX A PANCAKE

Mix a pancake,
Stir a pancake,
Pop it in the pan.

Fry the pancake,
Toss the pancake,
Catch it if you can.

Mime appropriate actions.

14. ONE, TWO, BUCKLE MY SHOE

One, two, buckle my shoe,
Three, four, shut the door,
Five, six, pick up sticks,
Seven, eight, lay them straight,
Nine, ten, a big fat hen.

15. HANDS ON HIPS

Hands on hips,
Hands on knees,
Hands behind you, if you please.
Touch your shoulders,
Touch your toes,
Touch your knees
And then touch your nose.
Raise your hands way up high,
Let your fingers swiftly fly.
Hold them out in front of you,
While you clap them, one and two.

16. HERE IS THE CHURCH

Here is the Church,
(Interface fingers with knuckles showing upwards.)
Here is the steeple,
(Point index fingers up together to make a steeple.)
Open the doors,
(Turn hands over with fingers still interfaced.)
And here are the people,
(Wriggle fingertips.)
Here is the Parson going upstairs,
(Make a ladder with left hand and walk thumb and finger up.)
And here he is a-saying his prayers.
(Put hands together as for prayers.)

17. JACK IN THE BOX, JUMPS UP LIKE THIS!

Jack in the box, jumps up like this,
And waggles his head from side to side.
Then I gently press him down again,
Saying, 'Jack in the box you must go to bed.'

*Commence in a curled-up position on the floor, knees tucked
underneath the body, head tucked in.*
*'Jack in the box, jumps up like this,' A large jump into the air with both
hands extended above the head.*
*'And waggles his head from side to side.' The head inclines to the right
side and to the left side. Repeat.*
*'Then I gently press him down again, Saying, ''Jack in the box you
must go to bed.''' Place the palm of the right hand on top of the head
and slowly bend the knees to finish curled up on the floor in the original
position.*

18. OLD JOHN MUDDLECOMBE LOST HIS CAP

Old John Muddlecombe lost his cap,
(Put hands on head.)
He couldn't find it anywhere, the poor old chap,
(Presume to look for cap.)
He walked down the High Street, and everybody said,
'Silly John Muddlecombe, you've got it on your HEAD.'

Shake finger at imaginary old man then put hands on head.

19. ROLY POLY, EVER SO SLOWLY

Roly poly, ever so slowly, ever so ... slowly,
Roly poly, faster, faster, faster, FASTER,
Roly poly, ever so slowly, etc.

Roll fists round each other.

20. PIGGY ON THE RAILWAY

Piggy on the railway,
Picking up stones,
Along came an engine,
And broke poor Piggy's bones.

'Oh', said Piggy,
'That's not fair,'
'Oh', said the engine driver,
'I don't care.'

One fist represents Piggy and the other the engine. Shake one finger admonishingly, then give a big shrug.

21. TEDDY BEAR

Teddy bear, teddy bear dance on your toes,
Teddy bear, teddy bear touch your nose.
Teddy bear, teddy bear stand on your head,
Teddy bear, teddy bear go to bed.
Teddy bear, teddy bear wake up now,
Teddy bear, teddy bear make your bow.

Can also be demonstrated using a teddy bear with children following his movements.

22. HERE IS THE DEEP BLUE SEA

Here is the deep blue sea,
(Hands making waves from left to right.)
Here is a boat,
(Make fists with both hands and touch little fingers together.)
And here is me.
(Lift right index finger from fist position.)
All bright fishes down below,
(Wriggle all the fingers in the sea.)
Waggle their tails and off they go.
(Fingers waggle from side to side 'swimming'.)

23. TEN FAT SAUSAGES FRYING IN THE PAN

Either

Ten fat sausages frying in the pan,
(Show ten fingers.)

One went pop and another went bang!
(Clap hands loudly.)

Eight fat sausages etc.
(Adjust number of fingers held up in each verse.)

No fat sausages frying in the pan,
Sizzle, sizzle, sizzle the pan went bang!

Or

Five fat sausages frying in the pan,
Sizzle, sizzle, sizzle one went bang!
Four fat sausages, etc.

No fat sausages frying in the pan,
Sizzle, sizzle, sizzle the pan went bang!

24. TEN LITTLE SQUIRRELS SITTING IN A TREE

Ten little squirrels sitting in a tree,
(Show ten fingers.)
The first two said, 'Why, what do we see?'
(Clench both fists, thumbs raised.)
The second two said, 'A man with a gun.'
(Point both index fingers forward to indicate gun.)
The third two said, 'Let's run, let's run!'
(Raise both middle fingers.)
The fourth two said, 'Let's hide in the shade.'
(Raise both ring fingers.)
The fifth said, 'Why? We're not afraid.'
(Raise both little fingers.)
But bang went the gun,
(Clap hands together loudly.)
And away they all ran!
(Hide both hands behind back.)

25. THE MARIGOLD SEED

I had a little marigold seed,
I put it in a pot,
And watered it and watered it,
With ginger pop.
It grew, and grew, and grew, and grew –
Until a balloon appeared on top!
Then one day … that balloon went pop!

26. THE WINDMILL RHYME

Way over there,
(Point into distance.)
On a very high hill,
(Raise both arms above the head with finger-tips touching.)
Stands a dear little Windmill,
(Cross fingers.)
And the wind goes,
Oooooooooh, ooooooooh,
(Blow on fingers.)
And the sails go round,
(Roll hands round.)
And all the corn for the miller is ground.
(Rub palm of hands round and round.)

27. TWO LITTLE DICKY-BIRDS

Two little dicky-birds,
(Use index fingers to represent birds.)
Sitting on a wall,
One named Peter and one named Paul.
'Fly away Peter, fly away Paul.'
(Hide appropriate finger behind back.)
'Come back Peter, come back Paul.'
(Return appropriate index finger from behind the back to the front.)

28. THESE ARE GRANDMOTHER'S GLASSES

These are Grandmother's glasses,
This is Grandmother's hat;
Grandmother claps her hands like this,
And folds them in her lap.

These are Grandfather's glasses,
This is Grandfather's hat;
This is the way he folds his arms,
And has a little nap.

Make appropriate actions to fit the words, joining fingers and thumbs to make the spectacles.
Use a deeper voice for second verse.

29. UP THE TALL, WHITE CANDLESTICK

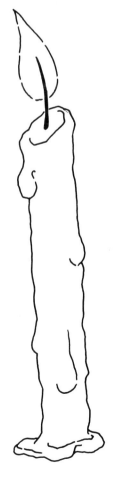

Up the tall, white candlestick,
(Raise left arm.)
Crept little Mousey Brown,
(Two fingers of right hand run up candlestick.)
Right to the top, but he couldn't get down,
(Fingers stay at the top.)
So he called to his Grandma,
(Call through cupped hands.)
'Grandma, Grandma.'
But Grandma was in town,
So he curled himself into a little ball,
(Raise left arm and clench right fist beside left hand.)
And rolled himself down.
(Clench both fists and roll round each other moving downwards.)

30. TEN LITTLE FINGERS

I have ten little fingers,
They all belong to me,
I can make them do things,
Come … and watch me.
I can shut them tight,
Or open them wide.
I can put them together,
Or make them hide.
I can make them jump … high,
Or make them jump … low,
I can hold them quietly,
And hold them, just so!

31. IN A CIRCLE, IN A CIRCLE, EVERYBODY IN A CIRCLE

In a circle, in a circle, everybody in a circle,
Holding hands, holding hands,
Everybody holding hands.
(Repeat.)
Walking round, walking round,
Everybody walking round.
(Repeat.)
Stamping feet, stamping feet,
Everybody stamping feet.
(Repeat.)
Clapping hands.
Nodding heads.

32. ONE, TWO, THREE, FOUR

One, two, three, four,
These little pussy-cats came to my door,
(Hold up four fingers of the right hand and count them.)
They just stood there and said, 'Good day.'
(Fingers bow on 'Good day.')
And then they tip-toed right away.
*(Walk the fingers away in front of the body and
over behind left shoulder.)*

33. ISN'T IT FUNNY HOW A BEAR LIKES HONEY?

Isn't it funny how a bear likes honey?
Buzz, Buzz, Buzz,
I wonder why he
Does, Does, Does,
'Mr Bear, Mr Bear, your honey's not there!'

The children sit in a circle with the child representing the bear in the centre, lying asleep with the honey pot beside him.
After the first four lines of the verse the child representing the 'honey thief' creeps up to the honey pot, picks it up carefully and runs around the outside of the group in the circle.
The bear wakes - 'your honey's not there!' - to find his honey pot missing and chases the thief, still running around the outside of the circle.
The thief, having run once around the circle, returns and places the honey pot in the centre.
The game is repeated with another 'bear' and a different 'honey thief'.

34. I WRIGGLE MY FINGERS

I wrig-gle my fin-gers, I wrig-gle my toes, I wrig-gle my shoul-ders, I wrig-gle my nose, now

no more wrig-gles are left in me, So I will be still, as still as can be.

27

Side 1A

35. CLAP YOUR HANDS TOGETHER, CLAP, CLAP, CLAP

Clap your hands to-ge-ther clap, clap, clap, Clap your hands to-ge-ther clap, clap, clap, Touch your knees, Touch your toes, Turn a-round and touch your nose. Clap your hands to-ge-ther clap, clap, clap.

v.2   Stamp your feet and make a noise,
        Stamp, stamp, stamp,
        Stamp your feet and make a noise,
        Stamp, stamp, stamp,
        Touch your knees, etc.

v.3   Tap your shoulders quietly, tap, tap, tap,
        Tap your shoulders quietly, tap, tap, tap,
        Touch your knees, etc.

28

Side 1A

36. OPEN, SHUT THEM

O - pen, shut them, o - pen, shut them, Give a lit - tle clap,

O - pen, shut them, o - pen, shut them, Lay them in your lap,

Roll them, roll them, roll them, roll them, Roll them just like this,

Shake them, shake them, shake them, shake them, Blow a lit - tle kiss.

Begin with clenched fists held in front, open and close fingers.

Side 1A **37. IF YOU'RE HAPPY AND YOU KNOW IT**

v.2   If you're happy and you know it, stamp your feet.
      (Stamp, stamp.)

v.3   If you're happy and you know it, nod your head.
      (Nod, nod.)

v.4   If you're happy and you know it do all three.
      *(Clap hands together twice, stamp feet - right foot then
      left foot, nod head twice.)*

*v.4 If you're happy and you know it shout 'Hoorah!'
      alternative

38. FIVE LITTLE TEDDY BEARS

Five lit-tle ted-dy bears bounc-ing on the bed, One fell__ off and bumped his head,

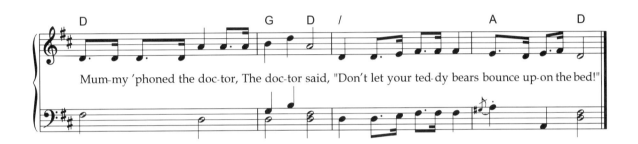

Mum-my 'phoned the doc-tor, The doc-tor said, "Don't let your ted-dy bears bounce up-on the bed!"

v.2   Four little teddy bears, etc.
(Four fingers 'bouncing' up and down.)
One fell off and bumped his head,
Mummy 'phoned the doctor,
(With the right index finger make two small circular movements; lift the right hand close to the right ear as if holding a telephone.)
The doctor said,
'Don't let your teddy bears bounce upon the bed!'
(Wag index finger – stern face.)

v.3   Three little teddy bears, etc.

v.4   Two little teddy bears, etc.

v.5   One little teddy bear, etc.

v.6   Five little teddy bears fast asleep in bed,
Each one has a bandage on his head.
Mummy tucked them in and said,
'No more bouncing on the bed!'

Maintain actions throughout all verses.

39. JACK IN THE BOX

Commence in a curled up position on the floor, both knees underneath the body, head tucked in close to knees.

'YES I WILL,' Take a large jump into the air, arms extended, fingers shaking; stand with both feet slightly apart.

40. LET'S ALL CLAP TOGETHER

v.2   Let's all stamp together, etc.

v.3   Let's all nod together, etc.

v.4   Let's all shake hands together, etc.

41. MY HANDS UPON MY HEAD I PLACE

My hands up-on my head I place, Up-on my shoul-ders, On my face,

At my waist, And by my side, And then be-hind me, they will hide, Then

I will raise them way up high, And make my fin-gers fly, fly, fly, Then

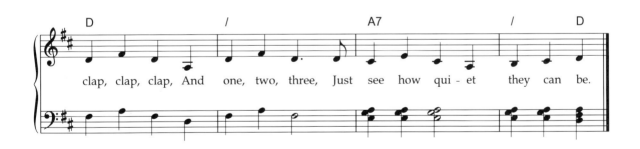

clap, clap, clap, And one, two, three, Just see how qui-et they can be.

42. RAINDROPS

Side 1A

43. ROLY POLY

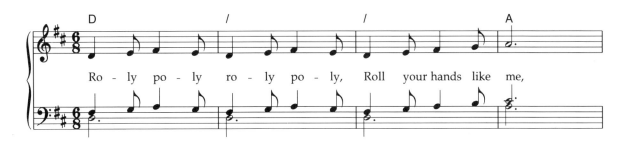

Ro - ly po - ly ro - ly po - ly, Roll your hands like me,

Roll them both to - ge - ther, And put them on your knee.

v.2   Roly poly roly poly,
      Clap your hands like me,
      Clap them both together,
      And put them on your knee.

v.3   Roly poly roly poly,
      Shake your hands, etc.

v.4   Wave your hands, etc.

v.5   Hide your hands, etc.

'Roly poly roly poly,' Roll both hands around each other with a forward circular movement.

Side 1A 44. SEE THE LITTLE BUNNY SLEEPING

See the lit-tle bun-ny sleep-ing, Till it's near-ly noon,

Come and let us gen-tly wake him, With a mer-ry tune.

Oh, how still, Is he ill? Wake him soon.

Hop, lit-tle bun-ny, hop, hop, hop,

Hop, lit-tle bun-ny, hop, hop, hop.

Children pretend to be sleeping rabbits.
Clap loudly after 'Wake him soon.'
Children then hop round room.

Side 1A — 45. ROUND AND ROUND THE VILLAGE

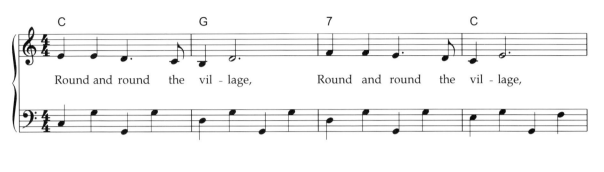

Round and round the vil-lage, Round and round the vil-lage,

Round and round the vil-lage, As we have done be-fore.

v.2   In and out the windows, etc.

v.3   Take yourself a partner, etc.

v.4   Curtsey/Bow before you leave him/her, etc.

One child skips outside the ring of children.
He/she then skips in and out, under their raised arms.
He/she then takes a partner and dances with her/him in the ring.
He bows, she curtseys and they both rejoin the ring.

Side 1A

46. I'VE GOT AN ENGINE

Finger and Action Rhymes

38

Commence kneeling on the floor.

'I've got an engine with wheels that go round,' Roll both hands around each other with a forward, circular movement.

'Zoom' Tap both thighs with the palms of both hands.

'Tic a Tac,' Clap both hands together, twice.

Repeat 'Zoom, Tic a Tac'.

'Zoom.' Finish with palms on top of thighs.

'With a bit that goes up' Raise right hand and arm above head.

'And drops down to the ground,' Lower right hand and arm to the floor.

Repeat 'Zoom Tic a Tac,' sequence.

'Up … Down' Raise and lower right hand and arm again. When sung a second time change right hand and arm actions to standing up and sitting down.

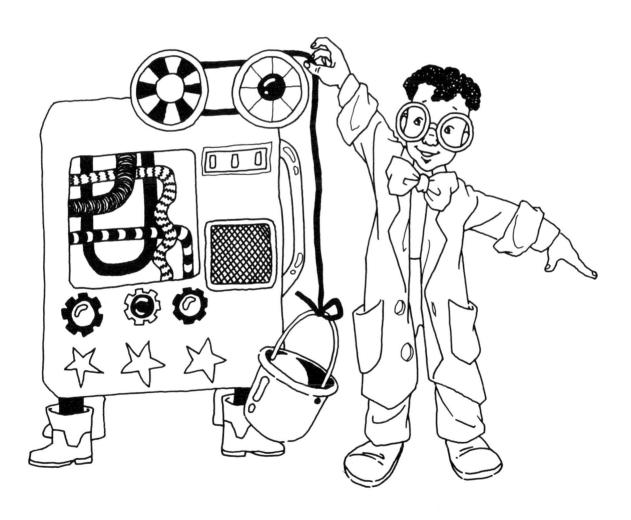

SONGS

1. THE ANTS WENT MARCHING

v.2   Two by two – stopped to do up his shoe.

v.3   Three by three – stopped to climb up a tree.

Can go as far as ten by ten, each time ask for or suggest something the ants can do which rhymes with the appropriate number.

2. AEROPLANES, AEROPLANES ALL IN A ROW

Side 1B

Ae-ro-planes, ae-ro-planes all in a row, Ae-ro-planes, ae-ro-planes rea-dy to go.

Hark they're be - gin - ning to buzz and to hum, (Bzzzzzzzzzz)

En - gines all work-ing so come a - long come, Now we are fly - ing up

in - to the sky, Fas - ter and fas - ter, oh, ev - er so high.

The children commence lying face down on the floor both arms extended to the side to represent aeroplane wings.
'Hark they're beginning to buzz and to hum, Bzzzz.' The children begin to hum.
'Engines all working so come along come,' The children rise to a standing position, both arms extended to the side.
'Now we are flying up into the sky, Faster and faster, oh, ever so high.' They move around the room - carefully avoiding other aeroplanes. Without musical accompaniment the children glide safely to the ground to finish in the original position, face down on the floor.

44

Side 1B 3. HERE WE GO ROUND THE MULBERRY BUSH

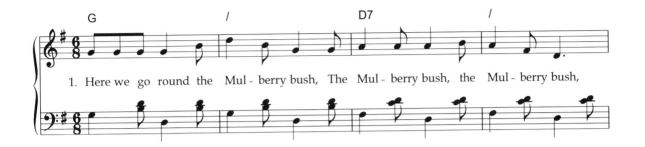

1. Here we go round the Mul-berry bush, The Mul-berry bush, the Mul-berry bush,

Here we go round the Mul-berry bush, On a cold and fro-sty morn-ing.

v.2   This is the way we brush our hair, etc.

v.3   This is the way we clean our teeth, etc.

v.4   This is the way we put on our coats, etc.

v.5   This is the way we do up our shoes, etc.

v.6   This is the way we walk to school, etc.

The children will suggest more actions.

4. FIVE LITTLE SPECKLED FROGS

1. Five lit - tle speck-led frogs, Sat on a speck-led log, Eat-ing the most de-li-cious grubs (Yum) (yum) One jumped in - to the pool, Where it was nice and cool, Then there were four green, speck-led frogs. (glub glub)

v.2   Four little speckled frogs,
Sat on a speckled log,
Eating the most delicious grubs
Yum, yum, etc.

v.3   Three little speckled frogs,
Sat on a speckled log,
Eating the most delicious grubs
Yum, yum, etc.

v.4   Two little speckled frogs,
Sat on a speckled log,
Eating the most delicious grubs
Yum, yum, etc.

v.5   One little speckled frog,
        Sat on a speckled log,
        Eating the most delicious grubs
        Yum, yum.
        He jumped into the pool,
        Where it was nice and cool,
        Then there were no green, speckled frogs
        Glub, glub.

The five frogs can be represented by using the five fingers of the right hand held up and placed on top of the clenched fist of the left hand – representing a log.
'One jumped into the pool,' The right hand and arm are fully extended high into the air on 'jumped' and lowered again on 'into the pool'.

OR: Five children can be chosen to represent the frogs. Small chairs or a bench seat can be the 'log', and a large piece of blue material on the floor makes a 'pool'. Frog masks are also fun to make and wear.

Side 1B 5. I WENT TO VISIT A FARM ONE DAY

Repeat choosing different animal sounds, e.g. a pig, a sheep, a cat.

Side 1B

6. FIVE CURRANT BUNS IN A BAKER'S SHOP

v.2   Four currant buns, etc.

v.3   Three currant buns, etc.

v.4   Two currant buns, etc.

v.5   One currant bun, etc.

v.6   No currant buns in the Baker's shop,
       Round and fat with a cherry on the top.
       Along came a boy/girl with a penny one day,
       'Sorry little boy/girl, no buns left today.'

'Five currant buns in a Baker's shop,' Commence using the five fingers of the right hand,
'Round and fat' Both hands and arms are lifted above the head and extended to the side using a circular movement.
'With a cherry on the top,' The palm of the right hand is lifted to pat the top of the head.
OR: This can be sung with a child chosen to be a Baker (wearing a baker's hat) and six pennies distributed to six children. A small table can be used as a prop to represent the Baker's shop.
The child chosen as the Baker commences by counting and placing each bun on the table (model clay currant buns with a cherry can be made by the children and used for this song).
Each of the six children given a penny listens for his or her name as it is sung in turn.

They exchange their penny at the Baker's shop for a currant bun and return to their place.
The child with the sixth penny listens to the Baker, 'Sorry little boy/girl, no buns left today', and returns sadly to his/her place.
To repeat the game the child unable to exchange the penny for a currant bun becomes the next Baker.

Side 1B

7. INCY-WINCY SPIDER

Use fingers of both hands to represent a spider climbing.
Raise hands and lower them slowly, wriggling fingers to indicate rain.
Lift both arms above head and open to the side with a circular movement.
As for first line above.

8. IN A COTTAGE IN A WOOD

'In a cottage in a wood,' The tips of the fingers of both hands touch to represent the shape of the cottage roof.

'A little old man at the window stood, Saw . . .' The thumbs and index fingers of both hands are lifted to encircle the eyes.

'A rabbit running by,' Both hands lifted to side and top of head to represent rabbit ears.

'Knocking at the door.' The right fist is clenched and lifted to strike 'the door' three times.

'Help' The fingers of both hands are placed lightly on the shoulders.

'Me!' Hands and arms extended above the head.

Repeat twice.

'Before the huntsman shoots me dead!' The left arm is held in front and across the body with right arm resting over the left wrist. The index finger of the right hand is pointed.
'Come little rabbit, come with me,' The right hand beckons with the index finger. Repeat beckoning movement three times.
'Happy we shall be!' The left hand is held resting in the lap with the index and middle fingers extended to represent rabbit's ears. The right hand strokes the back of the left hand gently three times.

9. FIVE LITTLE DUCKS WENT SWIMMING

Side 1B

1. Five lit-tle ducks went swim-ming one day, O – ver the hills and far a – way.

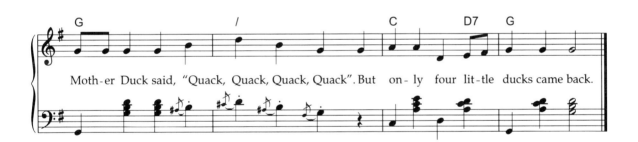

Moth-er Duck said, "Quack, Quack, Quack, Quack". But on-ly four lit-tle ducks came back.

v.2   Four little ducks went swimming one day, etc.

Last verse   One little duck went swimming one day,
Over the pond and far away.
Mother duck said, 'Quack, Quack, Quack, Quack',
And five little ducks came swimming back!

Songs

 Side 1B **10. OATS AND BEANS AND BARLEY GROW** ▶

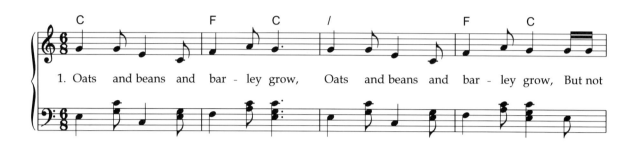

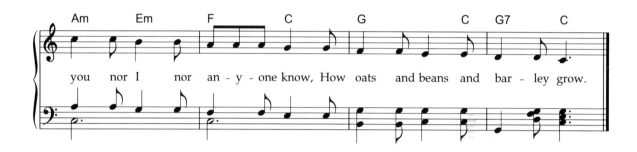

v.2   First the farmer sows his seed,
Then he stands and takes his ease,
Stamps his feet and claps his hands,
And turns around to view the land.

The children commence holding hands walking in a circle to the left. They release hands and stand with both feet placed slightly apart. The left arm is curved with the left hand placed on the left hip (a basket shape).

'First the farmer sows his seed,' The right hand scatters the seed from the basket, twice.

'Then he stands and takes his ease,' Both hands are placed on hips, both feet placed a little further apart.

'Stamps his feet' They stamp the right foot and repeat. They stamp with the left foot.

'And claps his hands,' They clap both hands together twice.

'And turns around to view the land.' They lift right hand as if shading eyes and turn to the right making a small circle.

They repeat walking in a circle to the right.

11. I HEAR THUNDER

I hear thun-der, I hear thun-der, Hark don't you? Hark don't you?

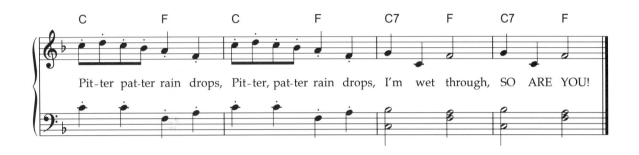

Pit-ter pat-ter rain drops, Pit-ter, pat-ter rain drops, I'm wet through, SO ARE YOU!

'I hear thunder, I hear thunder,' Commence sitting on the floor both legs extended in front with the heels of both feet drumming on the floor.
'Hark don't you? Hark don't you?' Raise the right hand to the right ear in the listening position (the palm of the hand faces forward with the fingers extended).
'Pitter patter rain drops, pitter patter rain drops,' Raise both hands and arms above the head and lower them with fingers 'wriggling' to represent rain-drops.
'I'm wet through,' Shake the shoulders and feel clothing with fingers.
'SO ARE YOU!' Point index fingers to neighbouring child/friend.

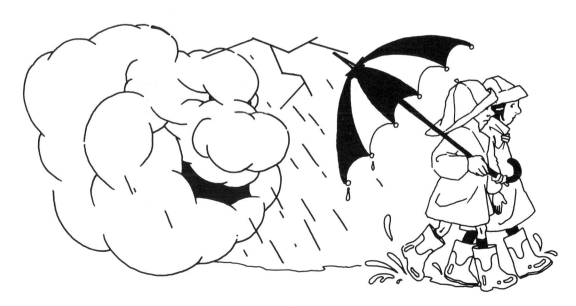

Side 1B
12. I'M A LITTLE TEA-POT, SHORT AND STOUT

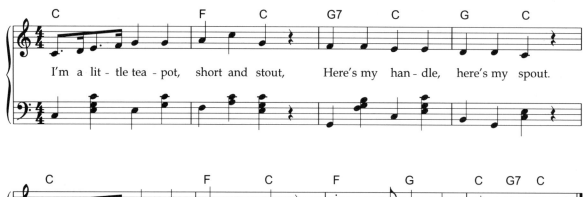

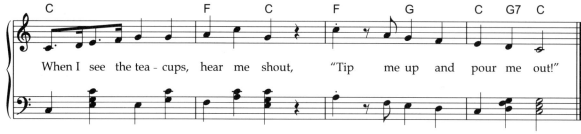

'I'm a little tea-pot, short and stout,' Commence standing with feet apart.

'Here's my handle,' The right hand is placed on the right hip.

'Here's my spout.' The left hand and arm are extended to the left side, the fingers together with the palm of the hand facing down.

'Tip me up and pour me out!' Bend the body from the waist slowly to the left side towards the extended hand and arm.

13. HERE WE GO LOOBY LOO

v.2   You put your left hand in, etc.

v.3   You put your right foot in, etc.

v.4   You put your left foot in, etc.

v.5   You put your whole self in,
You put your whole self out,
You shake it a little a little,
And turn yourself about.

The chorus is sung after each verse.

14. I WENT TO SCHOOL ONE MORNING

1. I went to school one mor-ning and I walked like this, Walked like this, walked like this. I

went to school one mor-ning and I walked like this, All on my way to school.

v.2   I saw a little robin and he hopped like this, etc.

v.3   I saw a shiny river and I splashed like this, etc.

v.4   I saw a little pony and he galloped like this, etc.

Allow the children to provide suggestions.

56

Side 1B

15. SIX LITTLE DUCKS

1. Six lit-tle ducks that I once knew, Fat ones, skin-ny ones, they were too, But the

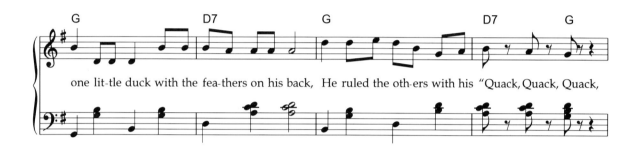

one lit-tle duck with the fea-thers on his back, He ruled the oth-ers with his "Quack, Quack, Quack,

Quack, Quack, Quack!" He ruled the oth-ers with his "Quack, Quack, Quack!"

v.2   Down the river they would go,
Wibble, wobble, wibble, wobble, to and fro,
But the one little duck with the feathers on his back,
He ruled the others with his 'Quack', etc.

v.3   Home from the river they would come,
Wibble, wobble, wibble, wobble, ho-hum-hum,
But the one little duck with the feathers on his back,
He ruled the others with his 'Quack', etc.

Side 1B 16. OH, THE GRAND OLD DUKE OF YORK

v.2   Oh, the Grand old Duke of York,
He had ten thousand men,
They beat their drums to the top of the hill,
And they beat them down again.
(chorus)

This can be sung introducing the marching step around the playroom and/or accompanied with the use of percussion instruments.

58

17. LITTLE ARABELLA MILLER

Little Arabella Miller, Found a woolly caterpillar.

First it crawled upon her mother, Then upon her baby brother.

All said, "Arabella Miller, Take away that caterpillar!"

Pretend to pick up the caterpillar; walk with the fingers of your right hand up your left arm, then vice versa. Pretend to pat the caterpillar.

59

18. LOOK WHO'S COME HERE, PUNCHINELLO

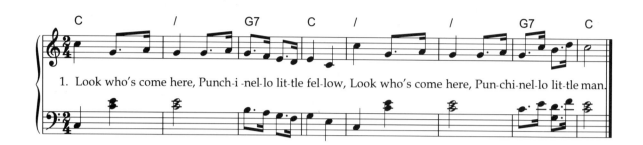

1. Look who's come here, Punch-i-nel-lo lit-tle fel-low, Look who's come here, Pun-chi-nel-lo lit-tle man.

v.2 What can you do, Punchinello little fellow?
What can you do, Punchinello little man?

v.3 We can do it too, Punchinello little fellow!
We can do it too, Punchinello little man!

'Look who's come here, Punchinello little fellow, Look who's come here, Punchinello little man.' Commence with the child chosen to be Punchinello standing in the centre of a ring of children holding hands and walking in a circle to the right.
'What can you do, Punchinello little fellow? What can you do, Punchinello little man?' Punchinello chooses an action – jumping, clapping, hopping, to perform on his own.
'We can do it too, Punchinello little fellow! We can do it too, Punchinello little man!' The children follow the same action Punchinello has demonstrated.

60

Side 1B **19. I LOVE TO ROW IN MY BIG BLUE BOAT**

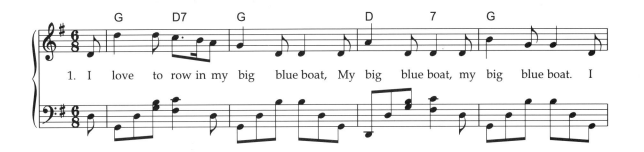

1. I love to row in my big blue boat, My big blue boat, my big blue boat. I

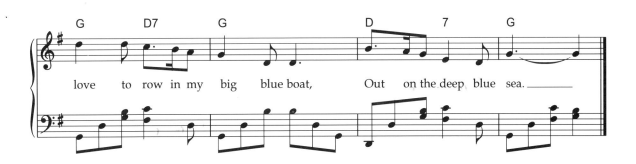

love to row in my big blue boat, Out on the deep blue sea.

v.2 My big blue boat has two red sails,
Two red sails, two red sails.
My big blue boat has two red sails,
Two red sails.

v.3 So, come for a row in my big blue boat,
My big blue boat, my big blue boat.
So, come for a sail in my big blue boat,
Out on the deep blue sea.

Verse 1 Commence sitting, both legs extended to the front and both hands held at waist level in front of the body – holding two oars. From the waist, bend forward and back, forward and back. Repeat three times.

Verse 2 Raise both hands and arms above the head and sway gently from the waist, to the right side, to the left side – raised arms representing the sails. Repeat four times.

Verse 3 As for verse 1.

20. HOKEY COKEY

v.2   You put your left arm in,
       Your left arm out,
       In, out, In, out and shake it all about.
       You do the Hokey Cokey and you turn around,
       That's what it's all about.
       (*chorus*)

v.3   You put your right leg in, etc.
       (*chorus*)

v.4   You put your left leg in, etc.
       (*chorus*)

v.5   You put your whole self in, etc.
(*chorus*)

Commence standing in a circle. 'You put your right arm in, Your right arm out, In, out, In, out and shake it all about,' Extend right arm forwards, then back; three times. Shake right arm vigorously.
'You do the Hokey Cokey,' Fingertips of both hands touch in 'roof shape'. Make a small tilting movement to the right side, left and right.
'And you turn around,' Release fingertips and make a complete turn to the right to finish facing into the circle.
'That's what it's all about.' Stamp right foot, left foot, right foot, clapping hands together three times.
'Oh, the Hokey Cokey,' Join hands together in the circle and advance to the centre and return. Repeat twice.
'Knees bend,' Bend both knees, hands on knees.
'Arms stretch,' Extend hands and arms above the head, straighten the knees.
'RA RA RA' Stamp right foot, left foot and right foot, clapping hands together three times.

21. RING A RING O' ROSES

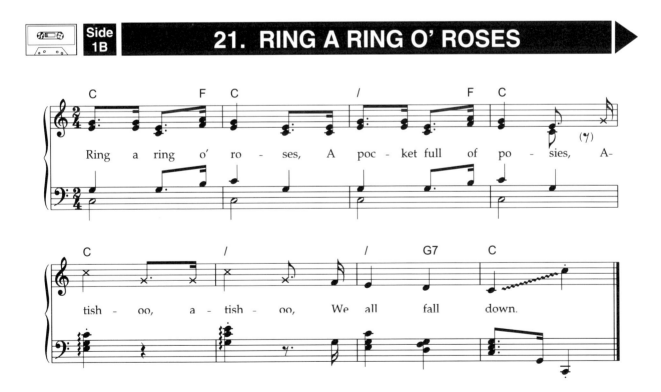

v.2   The cows are in the meadow,
Eating buttercups,
One, two, three, we all jump up!

22. DICE SONG

v.2   We've got three dots on top of the dice, etc.

A 'giant-sized' dice – made with a large square box, painted white with appropriate black spots – facilitates 'counting the dots', when sung with a large or small group of children. The verse depends on the throw of the dice.

23. THE MUSIC MAN

v.2   I play the drum.

v.3   I play the trumpet.

Children make suggestions. Instruments from the percussion collection can be used.

24. ROW, ROW, ROW, YOUR BOAT

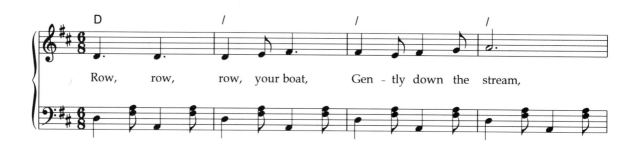

Row, row, row, your boat, Gen - tly down the stream,

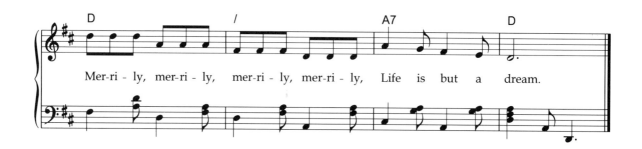

Mer-ri - ly, mer-ri - ly, mer-ri - ly, mer-ri - ly, Life is but a dream.

v.2   Row, row, row your boat,
Gently down the stream,
If you see a crocodile/alligator,
Don't forget to scream!

Two children sit facing each other on the floor, holding hands, and sway forwards and backwards.

Side 2A

25. THE FARMER'S IN HIS DEN

1. The Farm - er's in his den, The Farm - er's in his den,
E - I, E - I, The Farm - er's in his den.

v.2   The Farmer wants a wife, etc.

v.3   The wife wants a child, etc.

v.4   The child wants a nurse, etc.

v.5   The nurse wants a dog, etc.

v.6   The dog wants a bone, etc.
       We all pat the bone,
       Ee-aye-ee-aye,
       We all pat the bone.

Commence holding hands walking in a circle to the left, with the child chosen as the Farmer standing in the centre.
The Farmer chooses a wife, the wife a child, and so on.
As the small group in the centre increases they in turn hold hands and walk in a small circle to the left.
'We all pat the bone,' The small group in the centre pat the child representing the bone and the outer circle clap hands.

67

26. OH, WE CAN PLAY ON THE BIG BASS DRUM

Side 2A

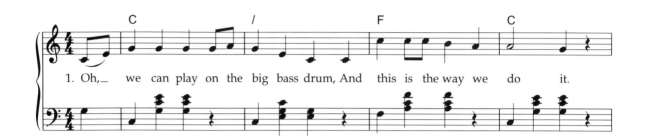

1. Oh,— we can play on the big bass drum, And this is the way we do it.

Boom, boom, boom goes the big bass drum, And that's the way we do it.

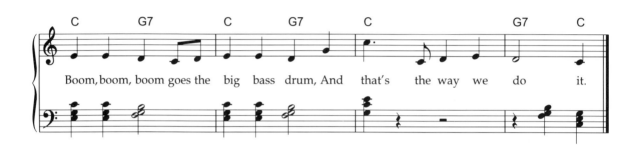

v.2   Oh, we can play on the triangle, etc.
       (tang, tang, tang)

v.3   Oh, we can play on the castanets, etc.
       (clack, clack, clack)

A selection of percussion instruments can be introduced in turn. Alternatively, stringed or wind instruments can be suggested by the children themselves.

27. JINGLE BELLS

Side 2A

Jin-gle bells, jin-gle bells, jin-gle all the way, Oh, what fun it is to ride on a

Side 2A **28. ONE FINGER, ONE THUMB**

One fin-ger, one thumb, keep mov - ing, One fin-ger, one thumb, keep mov - ing, One

fin - ger, one thumb, keep mov - ing, And we'll all be hap-py and gay.

v.2   One finger, one thumb, **one arm,**
Keep moving, etc.

v.3   One finger, one thumb, one arm,
One leg, keep moving, etc.

v.4   One finger, one thumb, one arm,
One leg, **one nod of the head,**
Keep moving, etc.

v.5   One finger, one thumb, one arm,
One leg, one nod of the head,
Stand up, sit down, keep moving, etc.

Side 2A **29. PETER HAMMERS WITH ONE HAMMER** ▶

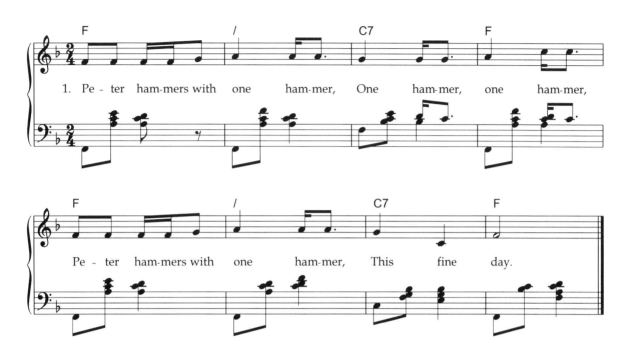

v.2 Peter hammers with two hammers, etc.

v.3 Peter hammers with three hammers, etc.

v.4 Peter hammers with four hammers, etc.

v.5 Peter hammers with five hammers, etc.

v.6 Peter's very tired now, etc.

v.7 Peter goes to sleep now, etc.

v.8 Peter's wide awake now, etc.

Commence sitting on the floor, legs extended in front.
Clench fist of right hand and tap the floor to the right side. Repeat three times.
Clench fist of the left hand and tap the floor to the left side.
With both fists tapping alternately, raise and lower the right leg simultaneously. Repeat three times.
With fists tapping alternately, raise and lower right and left leg alternately. Repeat three times.
Raise both fists and legs alternately with a nod of the head. Repeat three times.
Place both hands to the side of the left cheek, head resting in a tired position – inclined to the left side.
Lie back on the floor with eyes closed.
Sit up and repeat all movements simultaneously using a faster pace.

30. THE WHEELS ON THE BUS

1. The wheels on the bus go round and round, Round, and round, round and round, The wheels on the bus go round and round, All day long.

v.2   The horn on the bus goes peep, peep, peep, etc.

v.3   The windscreen wipers go swish, swish, swish, etc.

v.4   The people on the bus bounce up and down, etc.

v.5   The daddies on the bus go nod, nod, nod, etc.

v.6   The mummies on the bus go, chatter, chatter, chatter, etc.

Commence sitting in a ring on the floor. Both hands roll forward and around each other in a circular movement to represent the turning wheels.
Mime actions suggested by words, other suggestions may be contributed by the children.

Side 2A **31. WE ARE WOOD MEN SAWING TREES**

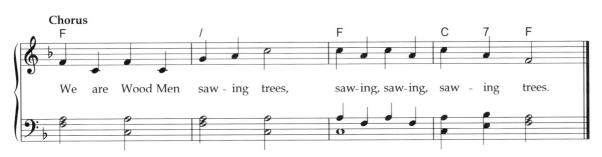

v.2   The trees fall down with a great big crash,
       Now we all will take the axe.
       And chop, chop, chop with all our might.
       To get some wood for the fire to light.
       (chorus)

v.3   Now we carry our logs along,
       Singing gaily this merry song,
       Tra-lalala, Tra-lalala
       Tra-lalala, Tra-lalala
       (chorus)

73

32. TOMMY THUMB, TOMMY THUMB

1. Tom - my Thumb, Tom - my Thumb, Where are you?

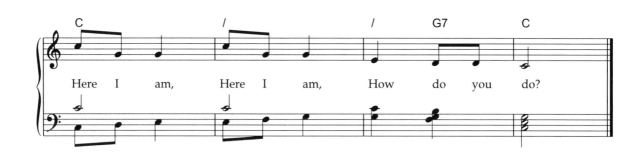

Here I am, Here I am, How do you do?

v.2	Peter Pointer, Peter Pointer, etc
v.3	Toby Tall, Toby Tall, etc.
v.4	Ruby Ring, Ruby Ring, etc.
v.5	Baby Small, Baby Small, etc.
v.6	Fingers (family) all, Fingers all, etc.

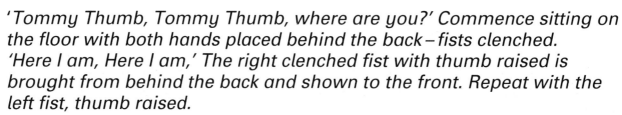

'Tommy Thumb, Tommy Thumb, where are you?' Commence sitting on the floor with both hands placed behind the back – fists clenched.
'Here I am, Here I am,' The right clenched fist with thumb raised is brought from behind the back and shown to the front. Repeat with the left fist, thumb raised.
'How do you do?' Both thumbs bend and extend three times – as if bowing. At the end of each verse both hands are placed behind the back.
'Peter Pointer,' Repeat with right and left index fingers.
'Toby Tall,' Repeat with right and left middle fingers.
'Ruby Ring,' Repeat with left and right ring fingers.
'Baby Small,' Repeat with right and left little fingers.
'Fingers (family) all, Fingers all. Here we are, Here we are.' Repeat with right and left hand.

Side 2A — 33. ONE LITTLE ELEPHANT BALANCING

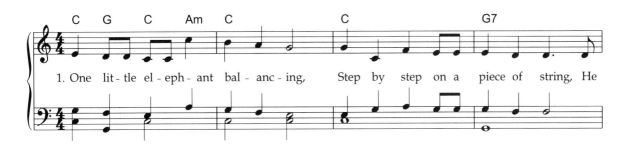

1. One lit-tle el-eph-ant bal-anc-ing, Step by step on a piece of string, He

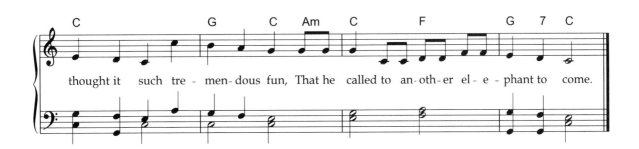

thought it such tre-men-dous fun, That he called to an-oth-er el-e-phant to come.

v.2 Two little elephants, etc.

v.3 Three little elephants, etc.

v.4 Four little elephants, etc.

v.5 Five little elephants balancing,
Step by step on a piece of string,
They thought it such tremendous fun,
But the string … it broke,
And they all fell down!

*A length of string is placed along the floor and held at each end.
The first child walks along the piece of string, arms extended to the
sides.
He or she returns to the other side and chooses a second child.
'But the string … it broke, and they all fell down!' Repeat until five
children walk along the piece of string and tumble to the floor.*

34. NOAH'S ARK

v.2   The animals went in three by three …
       The wasp, the ant and the bumble bee …

v.3   The animals went in four by four …
       The great hippopotamus stuck in the door …

v.4   The animals went in five by five …
       By helping each other they kept alive …

v.5   The animals went in six by six …
       They turned out the monkey because of his tricks …

v.6   The animals went in seven by seven …
The little pig thought he was going to heaven …

v.7   The animals went in eight by eight …
Some were on time and some were late …

v.8   The animals went in nine by nine …
Waiting patiently, all in line …

v.9   The animals went in ten by ten …
Five black roosters and five black hens …

v.10   Now Noah said, 'Go and Shut that door!
The rain's started falling and we can't
Take more'.

The chorus is sung after each verse.

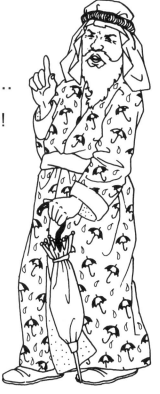

Side 2A

35. WHEN A DINOSAUR'S FEELING HUNGRY

When a di-no-saur's feel-ing hun-gry,___ He looks_ for food.___ He

looks in the for-est, ___ When he's in a hun-gry mood.___ When he

Make up, with the help of the children's suggestions, as many new verses as you like.

78

Side 2A 36. WE WISH YOU A MERRY CHRISTMAS

We wish you a Mer-ry Christ-mas, we wish you a Mer-ry Christ-mas, We

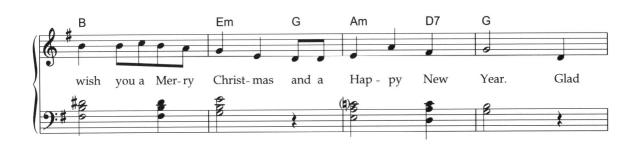

wish you a Mer-ry Christ-mas and a Hap-py New Year. Glad

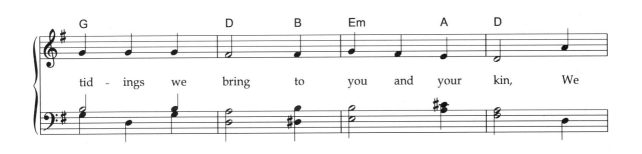

tid-ings we bring to you and your kin, We

wish you a Mer-ry Christ-mas and a Hap-py New Year.

37. THREE NAUGHTY KITTENS

1. There were three naugh-ty kit-tens, Climb-ing up a tree. Three naugh-ty kit-tens, One, Two, Three, Just see them climb, they ne-ver stop, Un-til they reach the top. Those three naugh-ty kit-tens, One, Two, Three.

v.2   Three helpless kittens,
Lost up a tree.
Three frightened kittens,
One, Two, Three,
And now they're up they can't get down,
Because they don't know how.
Those three helpless kittens,
Meow, meow, meow!

v.3   Here come three daring firemen,
Daring as can be!
Three daring firemen,
One, Two, Three,
Up the ladders, see them climb,
They saved them just in time,
Those three daring firemen,
One, Two, Three.

38. THE BEAR WENT OVER THE MOUNTAIN

The bear went o - ver the moun - tain, The bear went o - ver the moun - tain, The

bear went o - ver the moun - tain, To see what he could see. And

all that he could see, And all that he could see, Was the

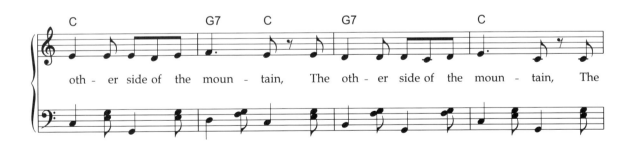

oth - er side of the moun - tain, The oth - er side of the moun - tain, The

oth - er side of the moun - tain, Was all that he could see.

39. HEADS, SHOULDERS, KNEES AND TOES

Side 2B

Verse 2   Omit singing 'Heads'.
Verse 3   Omit singing 'Heads, Shoulders'.
Verse 4   Omit singing 'Heads, Shoulders, Knees'.
Verse 5   Omit singing 'Heads, Shoulders, Knees and Toes'. No voices, only movements. Can be done sitting down on the floor, or standing.

40. LET'S MAKE A CAKE

v.2 *(chorus)*
And we will mix in the ice-cream,
Mix in the ice-cream,
Stir and stir and stir and stir.

v.3 We've made a cake,
We've made a cake,
Mixed in all the things that we like best,
A little bit of this,
A little bit of that,
Now we're going to eat it up.

Children make suggestions for the cake ingredients.

41. ONE POTATO, TWO POTATO

In my lit-tle gar-den, now prom-ise you won't laugh, I hav-en't an-y flow-ers and I

hav-en't an-y grass, But now I'm going to dig and plant, And soon I'll have a show; With a

bit of sun and a bit of rain, They'll be a lov-ely row of

One po-ta-to, two po-ta-to, three po-ta-to, four, Five po-ta-to, six po-ta-to,

sev-en po-ta-to, more. One po-ta-to, two po-ta-to, three po-ta-to, four,

five po-ta-to, six po-ta-to, sev-en po-ta-to, more.

42. THERE WAS A PRINCESS LONG AGO

v.2   And she lived in a big high tower.

v.3   One day a fairy waved her wand.

v.4   The Princess slept for a hundred years.

v.5   A great big forest grew around.

v.6   A handsome Prince came riding by.

v.7   He took his sword and cut it down.

v.8   He took her hand to wake her up.

v.9   So everybody's happy now.

'There was a Princess long ago,' One child is chosen to represent the Princess, another the fairy. Both commence in the centre of a ring of children, the Princess sitting on a chair, the fairy standing beside her. The children in the circle are kneeling.
'And she lived in a big high tower.' The children in the circle hold hands and lift their arms.
'One day a fairy waved her wand.' The fairy, holding her wand, dances and skips around the Princess.
'The Princess slept for a hundred years.' The Princess lies on the floor and closes her eyes.
'A great big forest grew around.' The children in the ring rise slowly from the kneeling position to stand with both arms lifted, swaying gently to the right and left.

'A handsome Prince came riding by.' The Prince with his sword gallops around the outside of the ring.

'He took his sword and cut it down.' With his sword the Prince touches each child in the ring until each one is sitting on the floor.

'He took her hand to wake her up.' The Prince enters the circle and awakens the sleeping Princess by lifting her hand.

'So everybody's happy now.' The Prince and Princess hold hands and dance, the children in the ring clap hands.

Side 2B

43. POSTMAN PAT

Post-man Pat, Post-man Pat, Post-man Pat and his black and white cat,

1. Ear - ly in the
2. All the birds are

morn - ing, just as day is dawn - ing, He picks up all the
sing - ing, the day is just be - gin - ning, Pat feels he's a

* to CODA (last time)

post - bags in his van.
real - ly luck-y man.

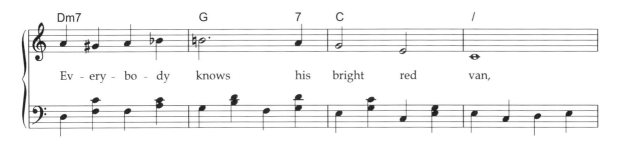

Ev - ery - bo - dy knows his bright red van,

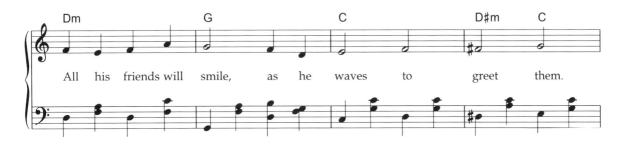

All his friends will smile, as he waves to greet them.

May - - be ..... you can nev-er be sure, There'll be

Back to beginning
with Repeat + Coda **CODA**

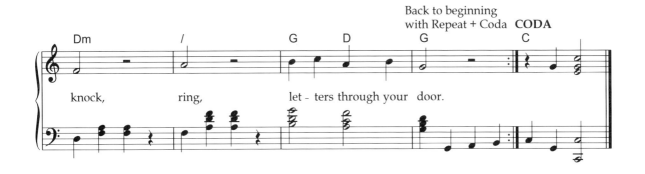

knock, ring, let - ters through your door.

 44. HOT CROSS BUNS

Hot cross buns, Hot cross buns, One-a- pen-ny, two-a- pen-ny,

87

Hot cross buns. If you have no daugh-ters, Give them to your sons, One-a-pen-ny, two-a-pen-ny, Hot cross buns.

Side 2B

45. HOORAH! IT'S CHRISTMAS

INTRO.

1. Let's jump in the air. Let's clap our hands. Let's

stamp our feet. HOO-RAH! (and)

IT'S   CHRIST-MAS!

shout   HOO-RAH!   and   shout   HOO-RAH!   IT'S   CHRIST-MAS!

v.2   Let's jump in the air.
Let's clap our hands.
Let's stamp our feet.
Hoorah!
and shout – 'Hoorah!
It's Christmas!'

v.3   Let's jump in the air.
Let's clap our hands.
Let's stamp our feet.
And shout
'Hoorah!'
and shout 'Hoorah!'
and shout 'Hoorah!
It's Christmas!'

*Verse 1 No singing at all, actions only. Jump in the air, clap hands,
stamp feet, hands in the air on 'Hoorah!', [Four bars intro.].
Verse 2 Children sing each line after teacher, [Four bars intro.].
Verse 3 Children sing and do actions at the same time, again following
the teacher.*

46. LITTLE TOPSY RABBIT

Side 2B

1. 'Little Topsy Rabbit' Commence with both hands placed at each side of the top of the head, fingers raised to represent the ears of the rabbit.

2. 'Had a fly upon her nose,' Both arms extended to the sides, raised and lowered twice to represent the wings of a fly, right index finger touches tip of nose.
   Repeat 1 and 2 twice.

3. 'So she flipped it' With the right hand lightly touch the nose to brush the fly away;
   'And flopped it,' Repeat movement with left hand.
   'And it flew away.' Repeat wing movements.

4. 'Shiny nose' With right hand touch the tip of the nose with small circular movements.
   'And curly whiskers,' Both hands rotate forwards at the side of the face with small circular movements.
   Repeat twice.
5. 'So she flipped it and flopped it, and it flew away.' Repeat movements as for 3.

Side 2B 47. I'M A DINGLE-DANGLE SCARECROW

v.2   When all the hens were roosting,
       And the moon behind the cloud,
       Up jumped the scarecrow, and shouted very loud.
       (chorus)

48. CHRISTMAS DAY

Chorus

On Christ-mas Day, Hey, Hey, Hey, Hey, We'll have a tree, Hee, Hee, Hee,

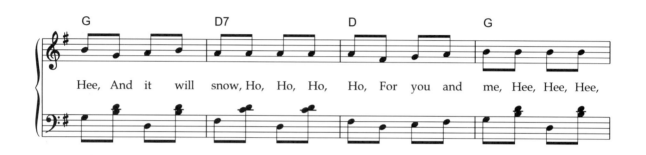

Hee, And it will snow, Ho, Ho, Ho, Ho, For you and me, Hee, Hee, Hee,

Hee. On Christ-mas Day, Hey, Hey, Hey, Hey, We'll have a tree, Hee, Hee, Hee,

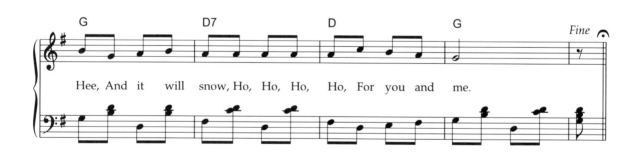

Hee, And it will snow, Ho, Ho, Ho, Ho, For you and me.

Verse

1. He wants a car, ___ He wants a car, ___

v.2   He wants a trumpet,
He wants a trumpet,
And he will go toot, toot, toot, etc.

He wants a car,
He wants a car,
And it will go broom, broom, broom, etc.

v.3   We'll all eat pudding,
We'll all eat pudding,
And we will go yum, yum, yum, etc.

He wants a trumpet,
He wants a trumpet,
And he will go toot, toot, toot, etc.

He wants a car,
He wants a car,
And it will go broom, broom, broom, etc.

49. MISS POLLY HAD A DOLLY

Miss Pol-ly had a dol-ly, Who was sick, sick, sick, So she 'phoned for the doc-tor, To be

quick, quick, quick. The doc - tor came,_ With his bag and his hat, And he

knocked _ at the door,___ With a RAT - A - TAT - TAT.

v.2   He looked at the dolly,
       (A 'sad' look at the doll held in the arms as before.)
       And he shook his head,
       (Shake the head to the right, to the left and right.)
       Then he said, 'Miss Polly put her
       straight to bed.'
       (Make seven pointing movements with the index finger of the right
       hand.)
       He wrote on a paper for a pill, pill, pill.
       (The right index finger 'writes' on the upturned palm of the left
       hand.)
       'I'll be back in the morning for my bill, bill, bill.'
       (Wave the right hand.)

'Miss Polly had a dolly who was sick, sick, sick,' Commence sitting on
the floor, arms rounded as if holding a doll.
'So she 'phoned for the doctor,' The right index finger makes two small
circular movements to represent dialling the telephone.
'To be quick, quick, quick.' With right hand close to right ear as if
holding a telephone.

94

'The doctor came, with his bag' The right fist is clenched as if holding the doctor's bag.
'And his hat,' The right hand taps the top of the head.
'With a rat-a-tat-tat.' The right fist is clenched and indicates knocking the door, three times.
This can also be sung with one child representing Miss Polly and another the doctor with a hat, bag and telephone used as props.

50. BANANAS IN PYJAMAS

95

51. MISTLETOE

Chorus

Mis-tle-toe, Mis-tle-toe, Mis-tle, Mis-tle, Mis-tle-toe, Adds to the Christ-mas cheer,

First you kiss some - bo - dy,__ And wish them a hap-py New Year.

Verse

1. First you kiss your hand, Kis - ses are for free,

Turn round to your friend, And put the kiss on their knee.

v.2 First you kiss your hand,
You've got a kiss to spare,
Turn round to your friend,
And put a kiss on their hair.
(chorus)

v.3 First you kiss your hand,
You don't have to speak, (shhhhhh ...)
Turn round to your friend,
And put a kiss on their cheek.
(chorus)

Side 2B

52. THERE WERE TEN IN THE BED

There were ten in the bed and the lit-tle one said, "Roll o-ver, Roll o-ver!" So they all rolled o-ver and one fell out.

Last verse

There was one in the bed and the lit-tle one said, "Good night!"

v.2   There were nine in the bed and the little one said, etc.

Continue until 'one in the bed' – last verse.

53. WHEN GOLDILOCKS WENT TO THE HOUSE OF THE BEARS

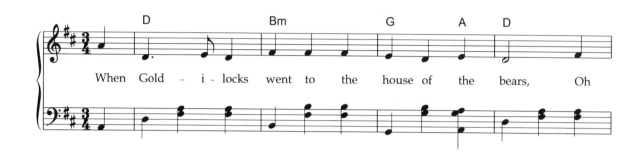

When Gold - i - locks went to the house of the bears, Oh

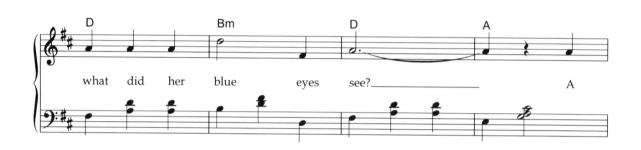

what did her blue eyes see?_____ A

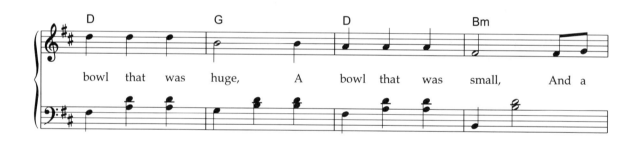

bowl that was huge, A bowl that was small, And a

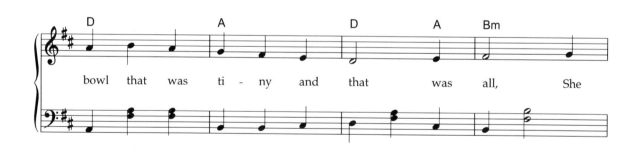

bowl that was ti - ny and that was all, She

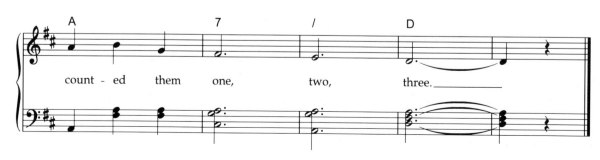

count - ed them one, two, three._____

v.2 When Goldilocks went to the house of the bears,
Oh what did her blue eyes see?
A chair that was huge,
(Extend right arm above head.)
A chair that was small,
*(Lower the right arm to shoulder level and hold the
palm of the hand face down.)*
And a chair that was tiny and that was all,
*(Lower the right arm level with the thigh, palm of
the hand face down.)*
She counted them, one, two, three.

v.3 When Goldilocks went to the house of the bears,
Oh what did her blue eyes see?
A bed that was huge,
*(Both arms extended to the side at shoulder level,
the palms of the hands facing each other.)*
A bed that was small,
*(Reduce the extension of both arms by tucking the
elbows in at waist level, forearms and hands held parallel.)*
And a bed that was tiny and that was all,
She counted them, one, two, three.

v.4 When Goldilocks went to the house of the bears,
Oh what did her blue eyes see?
A bear that was huge,
*(Stand up and extend both arms above the head,
feet apart.)*
A bear that was small,
(Lower both arms to the sides.)
And a bear that was tiny and that was all,
*(Close both feet together, bending both knees in a crouched
position, then sit on the floor with legs in front.)*
They growled at her, grr, grr, grr.
*(Lift both hands, fingers and thumbs, representing sharp
claws.)*

*'When Goldilocks went to the house of the bears,' Commence sitting on
the floor, legs extended in front, the fingertips of both hands held in
front and touching to represent the roof of the house.*
*'Oh what did her blue eyes see?' The thumb and index finger of both
hands touch to form two round shapes which are raised to encircle the
eyes.*
*'A bowl that was huge,' Both hands are held in front of the body –
palms held facing the body, the elbows are lifted with the arms
rounded to 'encircle' a huge bowl.*

'A bowl that was small,' Decrease the size by lowering the elbows and bringing both hands in towards the waist.

'A bowl that was tiny,' Both hands with fingers and thumbs touching to 'encircle' a tiny bowl.

'She counted them one, two, three.' The right fist is clenched, the thumb, the index finger, the middle finger extended in turn.

Side 2B — **54. WIND THE BOBBIN UP**

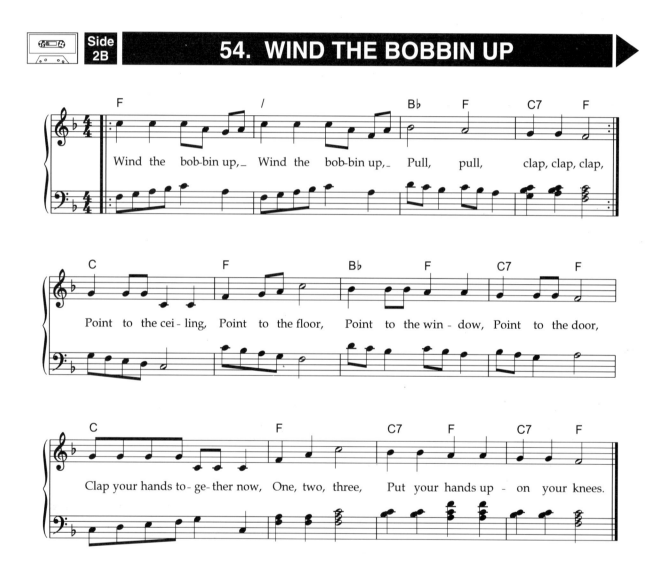

Wind the bob-bin up,_ Wind the bob-bin up,_ Pull, pull, clap, clap, clap,

Point to the cei - ling, Point to the floor, Point to the win - dow, Point to the door,

Clap your hands to-ge-ther now, One, two, three, Put your hands up - on your knees.

Commence with both hands rotating forward around each other.

Clench both fists and holding them in front, close together open to the side and close together.

Repeat. Clap twice.